HOCUS POCUS HOTEL

by Michael Dahl

illustrated by Lisa K. Weber

THE ABRACADABRA HOTEL

Contents

1

The not-so-secret meeting

Charlie Hitchcock needed a big, angry dog.

He needed a bodyguard.

He needed guts.

But, unluckily, Charlie didn't have any of those things.

Which is why he walked out of school at the end of the day to face his fate alone. Well, he was by himself, but he wasn't alone. Kids were lined up on both sides of the pavement, staring at him as he walked past.

"Good luck, Charlie."

"It'll be over soon."

"Remember, Hitch, tuck and roll."

"You're doomed, loser."

Both sides of the pavement were thick with kids who wanted to watch him leave school that afternoon. There were friends and well-wishers. There were kids who'd never heard of Charlie until that day, the kind of kids who went to car races hoping to see a crash. And there were enemies.

Slowly, Charlie trudged past them all. A few of them shook his hand.

One girl cried.

Another kid asked Charlie for his autograph.

"Maybe it'll be worth something," the boy explained. "After, you know, you're destroyed."

After more shouts of support, nervous whispers, laughs, and jeers, Charlie reached the end of the pavement. He sighed. Before he walked across the street, where he would be officially off school property, he turned around. The crowd had split apart, as his audience left the school grounds, moving away from him as quickly as they could.

Charlie shivered in the cold October breeze. He dug deep into his pocket and pulled out the piece of wrinkled notepaper he had been handed earlier in the day, between English and History classes.

The paper had been shoved into his hand by the biggest seventh-grader at Blackstone Middle School, Tyler Yu.

Ty had never spoken to him in the six years they had known each other. In fact, Ty never spoke to anyone. Charlie sometimes wondered if the biggest bully in school was able to speak at all.

Charlie had heard him yell, though, and grunt and shout. Because the one thing Tyler Yu did and did well, the one thing he was famous for, was fighting. His muscles and his temper were always getting him into trouble. After-school battles between Ty and other students were legendary. And they always started with a note.

For the thirty-seventh time that day, Charlie read the note.

MEET ME AFTER SCHOOL AT 1313 GIDEON STREET. ALLEY IN BACK. DON'T SHOW THIS TO ANYONE!!!!

So why had Ty picked on Charlie this time? And why had he given him an address for somewhere in the middle of the city? Ty's fights usually took place in the woods behind the school.

Thirty minutes of walking the busy streets of Blackstone brought Charlie to the alley behind Gideon Street. A blue neon sign shone near the entrance. The sign was in the shape of a top hat with a blue neon rabbit peeking out of it.

He should have gone home and hidden under his bed. That's what his best friend Andrew told him to do when Charlie showed him the note during History class. It was also what Andrew told everyone else when he spread the news throughout the school.

"I told him to go home and hide under his bed," Andrew kept saying. "But he won't do it."

Charlie couldn't help it. He may not have felt brave, but he wanted to see this thing through to the end.

Charlie looked up at the sign again.

The one thing that always drove Charlie nuts was not knowing the answer to a puzzle or riddle or secret. Charlie was curious, and Ty's note was a puzzle.

He had to know what it meant.

"Hey!" an unfamiliar voice muttered.

Charlie made out a tall shadow in the middle of the alley.

It was Ty, standing next to a big metal rubbish bin.

So that's why he told me to come here, Charlie thought. *So he could throw me in with the rest of the rubbish.*

Ty was wearing jeans, a T-shirt, his chain-wallet, and a pair of scuffed work boots. That was what he always wore. Along with a hard, sour expression.

He looks angry, thought Charlie. And he did. Even his spiky black hair looked angry.

Suddenly, Ty tossed open the lid of the garbage bin. The heavy lid swung back and struck the side of the brick building with a loud bang.

"Hurry up, Hitch!" ordered Ty.

Charlie walked closer. *At least the rubbish is in plastic bags,* he thought. *Maybe it won't smell so bad.*

"I said, hurry up!" Ty said. He lifted three giant bags of rubbish from the ground with one hand, as if they weighed no more than kittens. Without taking his eyes off Charlie, he slung the rubbish bags into the bin and slammed the lid shut.

Then Ty walked over to a door in the side of the brick building. He yanked it open and barked, "Inside."

Charlie did what he was told. The metal door slammed shut behind him.

He was alone in a dark room with Tyler Yu. This was it. The end.

In the dim light that leaked under another door, Charlie saw Tyler raise his fist.

Charlie wanted to close his eyes, but he didn't. He kept them open and braced himself for the punch. "What do you want?" he whispered.

Then he saw a finger poke out of Ty's fist.

"You," said Ty. "I need your help."

2 Abracadabra

Charlie was shocked. "You—?" he said. "You need my help?"

"Don't make a big deal out of it," growled Ty.

"But what do you want me to do?" asked Charlie. "And where are we, anyway?"

Ty pushed Charlie towards another door. He opened it, and then shoved the smaller boy into a large open space.

"Wow!" said Charlie.

They were standing at the side of a room as big as their school's gym. Tall marble pillars held up a distant ceiling of gold-painted shapes. A blood-red carpet covered the wide floor. Palm trees grew in giant pots, and enormous chairs and couches lurked in shadowy nooks and corners.

"It's just a hotel," said Ty.

"Wow," repeated Charlie. "It's not just a hotel. It's the Hocus Pocus Hotel. I've heard of this place."

"First of all, that's not its name," Ty said, his face darkening. "Secondly, it's where I live, okay? My mum's the hotel manager, and my dad's the chef. He's not a cook, he's a chef, got it?"

Charlie raised his hands. "I got it."

"We live over there, way back behind the

counter." Ty pointed to a wide marble counter, where two guests were checking in. A girl with dark pigtails and glittery glasses was helping them.

Other than the five of them, the hotel lobby was empty, although Charlie thought he saw a few shadows moving among the massive pieces of furniture.

Then he saw the painting.

The man in the painting wore a skinny black tuxedo and held a top hat in his left hand. The man looked young, with thick black hair, dark eyes, and a thin black moustache that ended in two enormous spirals. Behind the man was a woman with golden hair, lying inside a box, being sawn in half.

The painting hung near the entrance of the hotel. It was the first thing visitors saw as they walked through the front doors.

"Who's that?" asked Charlie, stepping closer for a better look.

"That's the guy who built this place," said Ty. "He's a magician. I mean, was a magician. Probably dead by now, I don't know. He disappeared or something. He built this place, like, a hundred years ago. He made it for other magicians to live in once they retired. But now other people stay here, too, like when they're on holiday or whatever."

"Magicians, huh?" said Charlie. That explained the blue neon sign by the alley, with the top hat and the rabbit. "Why does it say Abracadabra under this guy's portrait?" he asked.

"That's his name," Ty said. "The name of the hotel, too. The Abracadabra. Not the Hocus Pocus. Keep that straight."

Charlie shoved his hands into his pockets. He felt the folded piece of notepaper in one of his pockets and remembered why he was standing there in the first place. "So, what do you want me to do?" he asked.

Ty frowned. He grabbed Charlie by his shirt and pulled him behind a pillar. They were hidden by palm branches and giant vases.

Ty made a fist again. "Don't tell anyone," he ordered, "or this fist goes right through your face and out the other side."

"Tell what?" asked Charlie. "About the Abracadabra guy?"

Ty shook his head in disgust. He reached around for the chain-wallet in his back pocket and opened it. He pulled out a folded piece of paper – a picture torn from a magazine – and held it up to Charlie's nose. "See this?" Ty said.

"Uh, it's a dirt bike," said Charlie.

"Not just any dirt bike," said Tyler. "It's a Tezuki Slamhammer 750, Edition 6, in cherry-pop lightning red. And it's mine. Almost. I got money saved up from working here at the hotel."

Ty stood back and gazed at the picture. "I'm getting it as soon as school's out." He paused. "But not if you can't fix this problem."

"What problem?" said Charlie.

Ty carefully folded the paper and tucked it away. He stared hard at Charlie and said, "One of the magicians has disappeared."

3 Now you see him, now you don't

"Disappeared?" Charlie repeated.

"One of the old guys wasn't paying his bills," said Ty. "He's been staying here for years, but all of a sudden he stopped paying his rent. He's one of the retired magicians. Mr. Madagascar."

Ty looked around quickly, as if he were afraid someone might be listening. Then he motioned for Charlie to follow him past the potted palms and into an even darker corner.

They sat down behind a painted screen covered with dragons.

"I have a lot of jobs around here," Ty explained. "One of them is to pick up their rent once a month. If someone's late, I go talk to them and see if they're having a problem."

You probably scare them, too, thought Charlie. Ty was tall and muscular, and not someone to mess with or lie to.

"So I was supposed to go up and talk to Mr. Madagascar a few days ago," Ty went on. "But I didn't."

"Why not?" Charlie asked.

"I was in the middle of an epic battle in Empire of Blood, okay?" Ty said.

That was the first thing Ty had said that really made sense to Charlie. Charlie spent a lot of time after school on his own favourite game, Sherlock Holmes Maximum Z, an exciting detective mystery adventure. He understood how important it was to concentrate on a battle or investigation.

"I was slaughtering everyone," Ty said with a grin. "No one could beat me. There was no way I was stopping. In a few hours I finished the battle, and when it was done, I forgot about Mr. M. I didn't remember until the next day at school. So I rushed home and ran up to Mr. M.'s room, but he was gone."

"Maybe he'll come back," said Charlie. "Maybe he went on a trip."

"I don't think so," said Ty. "Come on, I'll show you his apartment."

Charlie followed Ty back into the main lobby. As they walked past the counter, the girl with the pigtails waved at Ty and said hello. Ty grumbled something and kept walking. The girl just smiled.

"Who's that?" asked Charlie.

Ty made a face. "Her name's Annie Solo. She works here in the afternoons," he said.

They stopped in front of a row of three elevators. The doors looked like they were carved from gold. Above each elevator, a gold half-circle with a golden arrow indicated what floor the elevator was on.

A bell rang and the elevator doors on the far left slid open.

"Our luck," said Ty. "It's Brack's elevator."

The elevator was lined in faded red leather. To one side stood a thin, elderly man in a maroon and black uniform. He smiled a wrinkly smile at Ty and Charlie.

"Good afternoon, Master Yu," the man said in a deep, clear voice. "A friend of yours?"

"This kid?" said Ty, nodding towards Charlie. "Nope. That's just Hitch."

"Short for Hitchcock," said Charlie. "Charlie Hitchcock is my name."

"Ah, like the famous director, Alfred Hitchcock," said the operator. "*Rear Window, Psycho, The Birds*. Among others, of course."

"What are you talking about?" asked Tyler.

"Hitchcock directed some of the world's greatest films," replied Brack. "He was the master of suspense."

"Yeah?" Tyler said. "Well, this Hitchcock is just doing a report for school about the hotel. I was telling him about the magicians and stuff. You know, that kind of thing."

The older man nodded slowly. "Ah, yes. One must beware the great Abracadabra Hotel," he said. "There is magic in its walls."

Ty chuckled. "Brack's always saying things like that."

"It is true, Master Yu," said the elevator operator. "Things happen here without explanation. Like the blackouts, for example."

"Blackouts?" Charlie repeated nervously.

The last thing he needed was to get stuck in an elevator with these two weirdoes if the electricity went out or something.

"It's nothing," said Ty. "Just a little problem with the lights. They went out a few times last week. But they're fixed now."

"Um, okay," Charlie said.

"That's not the kind of magic I meant, Brack," Ty said. "I mean, you know, the magical kind. Not the electrical kind."

Brack nodded. "Of course," he said. "But even the electrical kind seems more magical here." He smiled. "Young Master Hitchcock, have no fear about your report. Master Yu will tell you. This hotel was built by magic," he said. "Never trust what you see here. Or what you don't see. People may even seem to disappear from time to time . . . but remember, it's a big hotel."

Charlie wondered if the old man was referring to Mr. Madagascar.

A strange look came over the operator's face. "Now you see him, now you don't," he said, and pointed past them towards the lobby.

Ty and Charlie both turned to look, but the lobby was empty. When they turned around, the elevator was empty, too. Brack had vanished.

4 Magic and mirrors

"That's impossible," said Charlie.

"No, it's magic," said Ty. "It's the hotel."

The two boys stared at the elevator's interior. All Charlie saw was the faded red leather lining the walls.

The operator had vanished. But something about the walls didn't look right to Charlie.

"He didn't run away," said Charlie.

"Run away?" said Ty. "Brack?" He laughed. "I doubt it. He's too old."

A quiet chuckle echoed from within the elevator. Goosebumps ran up and down Charlie's arms. "That's him," whispered Charlie. "That's him, laughing at us."

"It can't be," said Ty. "He's not there."

Then they heard Brack's voice loud and clear. "Perhaps I'm standing right behind you."

The two turned again.

The huge lobby seemed to have grown more shadows, but no one was standing there. Annie was still over behind the counter, talking on the phone.

No one else was around.

When Charlie and Ty turned back to the elevator, Brack was standing there, smiling. "I told you," he said. "Never trust what you see here."

"Stupid magic," grumbled Ty.

Charlie's face lit up. "It's mirrors!" he exclaimed.

"What are you talking about?" said Ty.

Charlie hurried into the elevator.

"See this stain?" He pointed to a small stain on the back wall. It was about six feet from the floor. "It probably comes from people leaning against the wall," Charlie said. "The stuff in their hair rubs against the leather."

Brack's eyebrows rose up and his smile grew wider.

"But when Mr. Brack disappeared," Charlie continued, "this stain wasn't here."

"You sure?" asked Ty.

"Positive," said Charlie. He blushed and added, "My teachers say I have something called an acute visual memory. That means I remember everything I see."

"I know what it means," said Ty. "I'm not stupid. And I know about your photographic memory. Why did you think I picked you to help me?"

"I didn't say you were stupid," said Charlie. In fact, he figured someone who won epic battles in Empire of Blood was probably pretty smart. "I just mean that when Mr. Brack was gone, I didn't see the stain. And that means something was in front of the stain, hiding it."

"But we just saw the walls," said Ty.

"Right," said Charlie. "But not the back wall. We were actually seeing the side walls. Reflected on mirrors. It's an old magician's trick. Uh, no offence, Mr. Brack."

Brack applauded, clapping his faded gloves together. "None taken," he said. "Excellent reasoning, young man. Now, let me show you the actual trick, since you figured it out."

The operator reached out towards the walls on either side. There was a loud click. The two walls moved, swinging inwards.

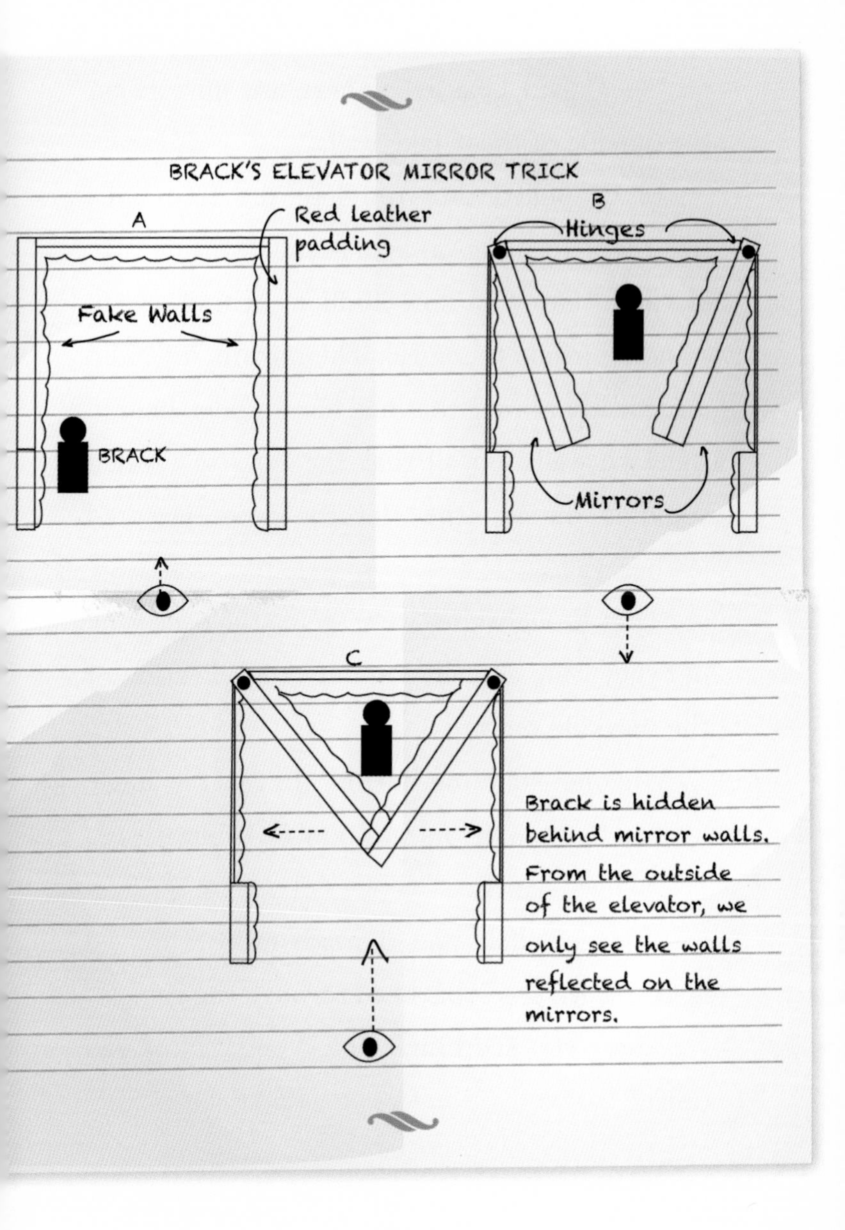
BRACK'S ELEVATOR MIRROR TRICK
A
Red leather padding
Fake Walls
BRACK
B
Hinges
Mirrors
C
Brack is hidden behind mirror walls. From the outside of the elevator, we only see the walls reflected on the mirrors.

"See?" said Charlie. "There are mirrors on the outside of those fake walls."

Brack pulled the fronts of the fake walls together, forming a small angle inside the elevator. He was now hidden behind them, standing inside the angle. The mirrors reflected more leather lining that had been hidden behind the fake walls. So all that the boys saw, when standing outside the elevator, were just red leather walls.

They thought they were seeing the back wall, but they were actually looking at a reflection of the two side walls.

Anyone standing inside the secret angle formed by the mirrors was now invisible.

"Wow!" said Ty.

Another click, and the two mirrors moved apart. Brack stuck his head through the gap.

"Now you see him," Brack said. "Now you don't."

Ty turned to Charlie. "That was great, Hitch," he said. "See? I knew you'd help out." He glanced at the elevator operator, who was watching them carefully. "Uh, take us up to Mr. M.'s floor, Brack."

"Of course, Master Yu," Brack said.

The two boys stepped inside the elevator, now back to normal, and watched as the doors slid shut.

5

The missing magician

As Ty led him towards a dim corridor on the fourteenth floor, Charlie turned to wave at Brack.

The elevator door in the middle of the row of elevators was already closing.

That's weird, thought Charlie. *Downstairs, Brack's elevator is on the left. But up here, Brack's door is in the middle of the row of elevators.*

"Hey," said Charlie, "did you know that—?"

"Yeah, yeah," said Ty, without bothering to stop. "The elevator moves sideways. Don't ask me how. It's magic."

"Yeah, no big deal, just some magic," Charlie muttered, shaking his head. "Okay."

They kept walking down the long hall, passing several corridors that branched off to the sides, leading into darkness.

Charlie tried to listen for people inside the rooms, but he didn't hear anything.

Not music playing, not a TV, not a voice. Not a breath.

It was like no one else was staying in the Abracadabra Hotel at all.

"Here's his room," said Ty.

They stopped at a door numbered 1413.

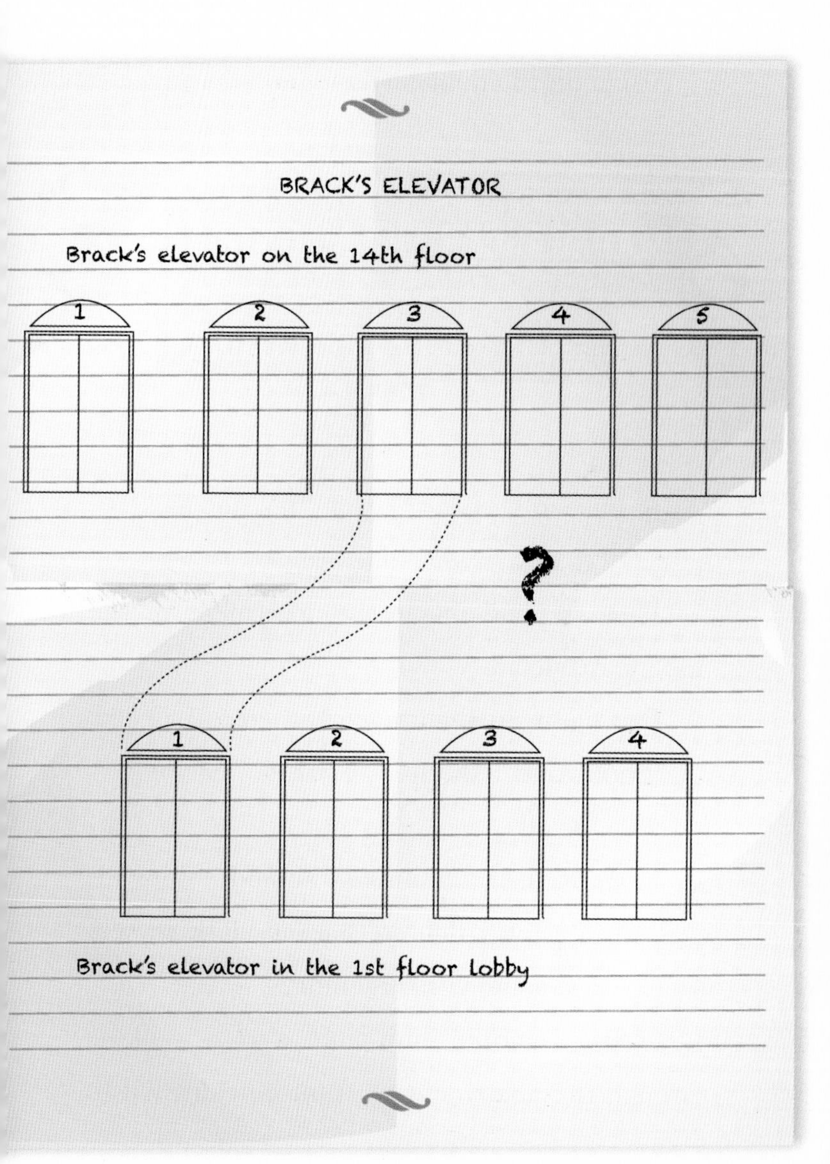
BRACK'S ELEVATOR
Brack's elevator on the 14th floor
1
2
3
4
5
?
1
2
3
4
Brack's elevator in the 1st floor lobby

A sign on the door read:

MADAGASCAR THE MAGNIFICENT

MASTER OF LEVITATION

Ty pushed the door open. "It's not locked," he said. "It wasn't yesterday, either."

They stepped inside the apartment of the missing magician.

Two figures rushed towards them.

"Look out!" shouted Charlie. "Someone's here!"

Ty snorted. "It's a mirror," he said, rolling his eyes. "And, wow, I figured that out all by myself. I must have acute visual memory."

Charlie ignored him and started walking through the apartment. A front corridor led to

a sitting room, a bedroom, a small kitchen, and a bathroom in the back. Most of the walls were covered with old posters from the days when Madagascar performed around the world.

Ty pointed out various objects as they walked through the rooms. "There's his suitcase, all his shoes, even his wallet," he said. "No one leaves their home without their wallet."

Charlie nodded. He saw a bunch of keys lying on a nearby table.

"Are those keys Mr. Madagascar's, too?" Charlie asked.

"Yup," said Ty. "See what I mean? He just vanished. I kept checking this place out all last night, but he never showed up."

"Why would someone leave without their keys?" Charlie said.

"Beats me," said Ty, scratching his neck.

Charlie walked back through the rest of the apartment. Although it was quite small, it

was very neat. Everything was in its place. Mr. Madagascar's rooms looked like the home of a very organized person.

In the front entry room, Ty stepped on something by the hall table. He bent down and picked up three plastic cylinders. "What do you suppose these are?" he asked.

Charlie looked closely. He stuck his finger through them.

Three empty tubes, about the size of his middle finger, maybe a little bigger.

Were they toys? Packages for sweets? They didn't seem like they'd be very useful.

I've seen these before, he thought. He was sure of that. But where?

"There's something printed on the side of them," said Ty.

Charlie held the tubes close to his glasses. Ty was right. "They're dated," said Charlie. "From last week. A week ago today, in fact."

"Let me see," said Ty.

Charlie handed them over, and then noticed something on the hall table. A manila folder like the ones his teachers used at school.

The folder was marked COME BACK. He felt a little guilty about reading someone else's private papers, but Charlie opened it up and began searching for clues.

Staring at the plastic tubes, Ty said, "Maybe the old guy likes sweets."

He gave them back to Charlie and then, suddenly, his expression changed.

"It's my fault I missed him," Ty growled. "I should have come up here when my mum told

me. Now I won't get my money this month." Ty pounded the wall with his fist. His face turned red.

No rent.

No money.

No Tezuki Slamhammer 750.

Charlie was sure that would be the end of his partnership with Ty. Surely the bully would demolish him now.

Suddenly, the lights flickered off and on.

"Not again," Ty groaned.

The lights went out, this time for several seconds. "This is not good," said Ty.

When the lights came back on, Charlie was staring at the mirror. Another face was staring back at him. An old man's face with bulging eyes and an open mouth. The man's head had poked through the open door behind them.

"That's him!" yelled Ty. "That's Mr. Madagascar!"

Then the man's face disappeared.

6 The open window

The two boys darted out the door.

"Where'd he go?" shouted Charlie.

"This way!" yelled Ty.

Charlie followed Ty through a maze of long, endless corridors. Corridors split off into more corridors. Every now and then they had to travel up or down a short flight of steps.

The sound of footsteps ahead of them was their only guide through the maze. Then the footsteps stopped.

"Did we lose him?" asked Charlie.

Ty shook his head. "I don't know," he said.

A cold October breeze passed down the hall. Somewhere, a window was open.

Without warning, Ty shouted angrily and banged his fist against a wall. "What an idiot!" he muttered.

Then a door nearby creaked open. A woman's voice called out, "What's all this ruckus? What's going on?"

The two boys followed the voice and turned a corner.

An older woman stood leaning against a doorframe with her hands on her hips. Light spilled from her room and glittered on the fancy

red bathrobe wrapped tightly around her. Her silver hair was piled high on her head.

"Is that you, Tyler?" she said. Charlie noticed that the woman's cheeks were bright pink.

"Sorry, Miss Drake," replied Ty. "We've been chasing someone."

"Chasing someone?" she cried. "Heavens to Betsy. I thought the hotel was falling down, with all that noise."

Ty introduced Charlie to the woman. Dotty Drake had once worked with magic herself. She had been a magician's assistant. "One of the best," she said, smiling.

"Were you sawn in half, or did you float through the air?" Charlie asked.

"A little of both," said Miss Drake.

"Sorry to butt in, Miss D., but did you hear anyone else run past your apartment tonight?" asked Ty.

"I heard lots of running," said the woman. "But who would be running around here?"

She stopped. She raised a hand to her mouth.

The lights flickered off and on again.

"Him . . ." she said faintly. With her other hand she pointed back down the corridor, behind the boys.

Charlie turned and saw a shadowy figure standing near the middle of the corridor.

"Mr. Madagascar," called Ty. "Is that you?"

The figure shouted back. "I'm sorry, young man. But I have to do this."

"What's going on?" said Miss Drake.

The lights flickered off and on. Miss Drake screamed and fell to the floor. "Oh no!" yelled Charlie. He and Ty knelt down beside her.

The lights turned off for several more seconds. When they came back on, the older woman's eyes fluttered.

"You must stop him," she said.

The boys looked back down the hall. The shadowy man was now standing at the far end, next to an open window. A breeze was blowing the purple curtains that hung on either side of the window.

"Wait!" cried Ty. "Mr. M.! What are you doing?"

Then, as Charlie watched, not believing his eyes, the man called Mr. Madagascar took a running start and leaped headfirst through the open window into the darkness beyond.

7 The master of levitation

Miss Drake screamed again.

Ty jumped up and hurried down the long corridor. Just as he passed another corridor, a second shadowy figure appeared. It collided with Ty. A shudder passed down the corridor. Then Ty groaned and collapsed, and the lights continued to flicker off and on.

At the far end, the window still stood open. The purple curtains rustled in the night wind. The sound of cars and traffic floated up from the streets below.

Charlie ran to the middle of the hall. "Ty, are you okay?" he asked.

In the darkness, Ty mumbled, "Where is he?"

The lights turned back on. Charlie ran over to the open window. He brushed aside the waving curtains and leaned out.

Far below on the pavement, people walked along as if nothing had happened. The outside of the building was smooth. The nearest windows were closed. It was a straight shot down, at least a dozen stories to the ground. There was no ledge, no roof, no awning, nothing that would have slowed down, or caught the body of the falling Mr. Madagascar. Where was he?

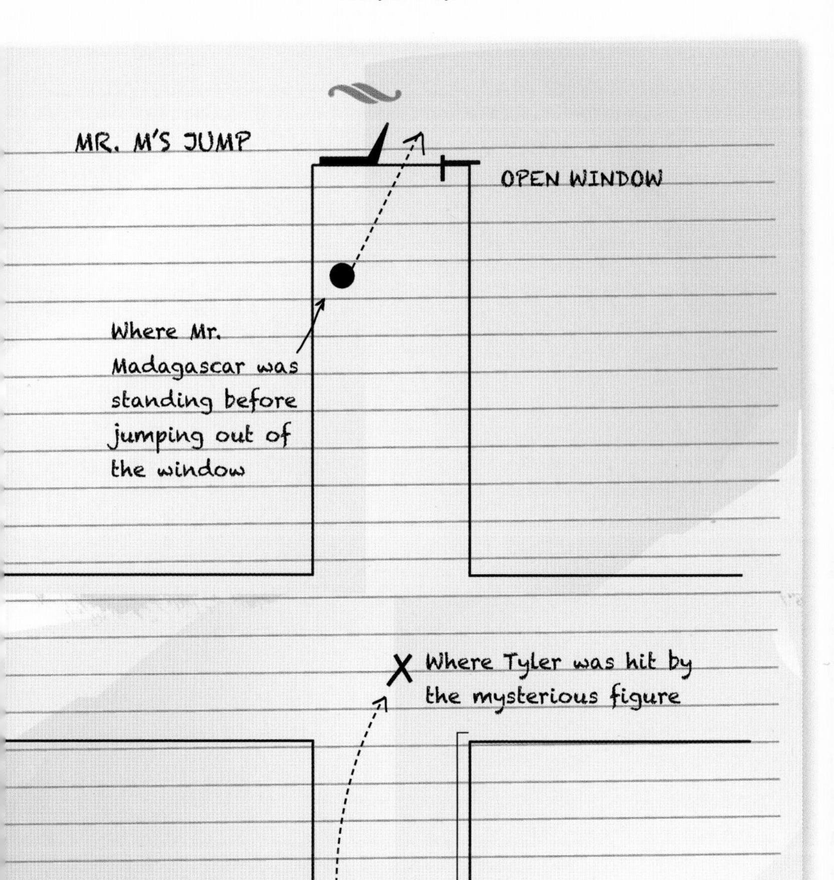
MR. M'S JUMP
OPEN WINDOW
Where Mr. Madagascar was standing before jumping out of the window
Where Tyler was hit by the mysterious figure
DOTTY DRAKE'S ROOM
TYLER
CHARLIE
DOTTY
THE CORRIDOR OF THE 14TH FLOOR

Miss Drake joined Charlie at the open window and looked out cautiously. The breeze tugged at her silver hair.

"What happened?" she asked. "Where is he?"

"Gone," said Charlie.

Miss Drake's face turned pale. Charlie was afraid she was going to faint again.

"That's impossible, young man," she said.

"Even for a magician?" asked Charlie.

The older woman stared hard at him. There was a glint of steel in her eyes. "Maybe not," she said. She looked at the pavement far below. Then her gaze wandered to the buildings across the street. "He was the Master of Levitation, after all," she said.

"But that's just fake magic," said Charlie. "I mean, it was a trick, right?"

"A trick?" asked Miss Drake, leaning out the window for a final look. "Well, if it was a trick, then it was the greatest magic trick in the world. Madagascar would be the first human to fly!"

That's impossible, Charlie thought. But a little voice inside him added, *Or is it?*

Miss Drake adjusted her red bathrobe, and Charlie noticed that it matched the waving curtains behind her. *That's funny,* thought Charlie. *I thought the curtains were purple.*

Miss Drake said, "We need to take Tyler downstairs."

Ty was sitting on the carpet, holding his head in his hands. "Where is he?" he mumbled again.

"Mr. Madagascar jumped out the window," said Charlie. "Um, do you think you might have concussion?"

Ty shook his head. "No, I mean the guy who ran into me."

In the craziness, Charlie had forgotten all about that second figure. The lights had been going off and on then. The shadowy stranger must have escaped during a blackout.

"I didn't get a good look at him," said Ty. "He looked tough, though."

"I didn't see him either," said Charlie. He looked closer at Ty and added, "You look terrible." Ty's face was covered in bruises. "You two really banged into each other."

"That should make him easy to find," said Ty, slowly getting to his feet. "Keep your eyes open for some jerk who looks like me, covered in bruises."

"Let's get you downstairs," said Miss Drake.

8
These crazy magicians

Mrs. Yu was upset when Ty and Charlie walked into the Yu family home, a small apartment tucked away behind the lobby.

"Tyler! I've been looking everywhere for you," she cried. As soon as she gave her son a closer look, she screamed. "Look at your face!" she yelled. "What happened to you? Go wash that blood off in the bathroom. And who is your friend?"

"This is just a kid from school," Ty said. "And I'm okay," he added.

"Does this have anything to do with Mr. Madagascar?" Mrs. Yu asked.

"Um, sort of," Ty said. "He jumped out the window."

Mrs. Yu shrieked. "I'm calling the police!" she said. "These crazy magicians—"

Ty hurried Charlie down the hall as Mrs. Yu ran into the kitchen.

In the bathroom, Charlie helped Ty wash crusted blood off his forehead. "I do look terrible," said Ty, staring into the mirror.

"You look like you ran into a wall," said Charlie. "A couple of walls."

Ty snorted. "Well, man, it's all over. I can't

get rent money from a guy who jumped out a window. Even if he is a magician."

Charlie looked at Ty's reflection in the mirror. "I'm not so sure of that," he said.

"That he's a magician? He definitely is," Ty said.

"No," Charlie said. "That he really jumped out the window."

"Are you kidding?" said Ty. He balled a towel up tightly in his fist. "Madagascar jumped out that window. We both saw him."

"We need to go back upstairs," said Charlie. "Before the police get here. We need to examine the scene of the crime. And," he added, "we need to figure out what these are." He pulled the strange plastic tubes from Madagascar's apartment out of his pocket.

"And figure out what those dates on them mean," said Ty.

"The dates are from one week ago today,"

said Charlie. "And didn't you say the lights were blinking off and on last week, too?"

Ty nodded thoughtfully. "Hey, have you noticed that the lights aren't blinking anymore?" he said.

Good call, thought Charlie.

In fact, the lights had stopped flickering ever since Mr. Madagascar jumped. Was the blinking light somehow connected to the magician's disappearance?

"Okay, let's go back," said Tyler, throwing down the towel. "Come on."

Clues and cents

Tyler and Charlie ran down a corridor behind the Yus' apartment.

"There's a way back to the elevators around here," called Ty.

When they got to the bank of elevators, Mr.

Brack's car was open. The boys quickly rushed inside.

"The fourteenth floor?" asked the operator. Charlie was silent. He was busy thinking of all the clues in this puzzle.

"Hey, Hitch," said Ty. "We're going back to Mr. M's, right?"

The old elevator operator leaned towards Charlie and grinned. "A penny for your thoughts, Master Hitchcock."

Penny? thought Charlie.

Yes, pennies made sense!

"Wait!" he said. "All the stuff I've seen tonight. It's all smooshed together like a jigsaw puzzle. You know that the teachers said I had a—"

"Yeah, yeah," said Ty. "A photographic memory. Acute visual whatever. I get it."

"Exactly," Charlie said. "So here's what we definitely know." He made a list of all the clues they'd come across that night.

1. The plastic tubes in Mr. M's room

2. The folder on his table

3. Brack's vanishing trick in the elevator

4. Brack saying that the hotel had magic ?? in its walls

5. The blackouts one week ago → suspicious

6. The colour of the curtains of the window Mr. M. jumped out of. Red? Purple?

7. The colour of Miss Drake's robe, and Miss Drake's scream

8. The neon sign of the rabbit and the hat outside the hotel

"What does the sign have to do with anything?" Ty asked. "And the colour of the curtains was purple. At least I think that's what I saw before I got knocked down. Let's go back up and check."

"Not yet," said Charlie. "We need to go to the basement."

Mr. Brack kept grinning, and down the elevator zoomed. At the bottom, the boys found themselves in the huge cellar and power centre of the hotel. "Where are the fuses?" asked Charlie.

Ty led him to a small room at the back of the cellar. The walls of the room were lined with old metal boxes. The boxes all hung about four feet above the damp floor. It reminded Charlie of a miniature locker room. On the closed doors of the metal boxes were labels: First Floor, Second Floor, and so on.

"I thought they'd have the old ones down here," said Charlie. "We need to find the fuse box for the fourteenth floor."

2ND FLOOR
3RD FLOOR
4TH FLOOR
9TH FLOOR
10TH FLOOR

After a few minutes of searching, and reading faded numbers on the boxes, Ty found the right one. "Here it is," he said.

"Did you have to come down here last week to check on things? When the power went out?" asked Charlie.

"No, the problem didn't last that long," Ty said. "It came back on by itself. We thought maybe it was the thunderstorm that night."

Charlie carefully opened the fuse box. Dust covered everything . . . except for some small round shapes on the bottom lip of the box.

As Ty took a step closer, his shoe crunched on something. He bent down. "Hey, it's another one of those plastic tubes," he said.

"And I'll bet if you look around, you'll even find a few pennies," said Charlie. "It's an old trick."

It was a good thing he spent so much time playing *Sherlock Holmes Maximum Z*. The penny trick had been used by one of the criminals he'd faced in the game. Then he'd done a bunch of Internet research on it, because he thought it was cool.

Charlie went on, "But the trick only works on old fuse boxes like these that have the old glass fuses. If you put a penny next to the fuse, it can cause it to short out, or flicker. That's what was in those plastic tubes. When you go to the bank and get change, you get it wrapped in those things."

"Oh yeah. I've seen people use them at cash registers when they run out of change," said Ty.

"So someone was causing those blackouts on purpose," said Charlie. "These circles where there isn't any dust? That's where someone put a stack of pennies. In fact, since the pennies were bought last week – the tubes had the date stamped on them, remember? – it means someone was planning for the lights going out."

"Ha! And I thought they were for sweets and he had a sweet tooth," said Ty. "So how did you figure out the penny thing?"

"I'd seen those plastic tubes before, but couldn't remember where," said Charlie. "Then when Brack said 'A penny for your thoughts' it all came together."

"Huh. Pretty smart, Hitch," said Ty.

Brack doesn't miss much, thought Charlie. *It's almost like he knows everything that's going on in the hotel. But now we need to go—*

"I think we need to go back to the fourteenth floor," said Ty.

"You read my mind," said Charlie.

10
Magic in the walls

Tyler and Charlie knocked on Dotty Drake's apartment door. They heard noises behind the door and then a voice. "It's very late. Who is it?"

"It's me again," said Ty. "Tyler Yu. Sorry to bother you, but it's very important."

The door opened slowly. Dotty Drake stood there, wrapped in her red robe.

"I was asleep," she said, yawning, patting her pile of hair.

Charlie noticed that the woman's cheeks were still pink. "Are you wearing make-up, Miss Drake?" he asked.

Miss Drake's eyes grew wide. "What on earth are you—"

"You said you were asleep, but you're wearing make-up," Charlie said. "Just like you were when we first saw you."

"Artists always wear make-up," she sputtered.

"When they sleep?" said Charlie. "I think you were wearing make-up because you were expecting company. And I don't think you were sleeping just now, either."

"Tyler, your friend is an insulting little boor," said Miss Drake.

"And I think you know what happened to Mr. Madagascar," said Charlie.

“I am going back to bed!” said Miss Drake. She tried to shut the door, but Charlie stopped her.

“The police are coming,” said Charlie. “The Yus are calling them. Don’t you want to hear what I have to say before they get here?”

“I don’t know what you’re talking about,” Miss Drake said.

“Just come over to the window,” said Charlie.

The three of them walked down the corridor to the window where Mr. Madagascar had jumped out.

Charlie raised his eyebrow at Ty.

"Yeah, I see it now," said Ty. "The curtains are red. They match the colour of Miss Drake's bathrobe."

"So?" Miss Drake said.

"That's right," said Charlie. "When you and I came over to the window and saw that Mr. M. had vanished, I saw that your gown matched the curtains. Red. In fact, if you look, all the curtains in the corridor windows are red. But when Mr. Madagascar jumped out the window, they were purple."

"You must be mistaken," said Miss Drake.

"No, I saw it too," said Ty.

"So then I wondered how red curtains could turn purple," said Charlie. He walked back down the corridor towards the intersection where Ty had been hit.

Then Charlie turned to his left and walked down that side corridor. He stopped at the end, next to its window.

"Look at these," said Charlie. Ty ran up to him. Miss Drake slowly followed.

"Purple!" said Ty. "But how?"

The boys leaned out the window. To the right, they saw the blue neon sign of the rabbit and the magician's hat. "Blue and red make purple," said Charlie.

"And look down there," said Ty. A few feet below the window was a wide ledge that ran along that side of the hotel. "If someone jumped out this window, they'd land on that ledge."

"But we all thought he jumped out the other window," said Charlie. "Where there was a straight drop to the street."

"It was an amazing magic trick," said Dotty.

"Yes, it was," said Charlie. "But not a trick of levitation, or floating. It was a trick with mirrors."

"Just like Brack's trick in the elevator," said Ty, nodding.

"Brack said the hotel's walls were full of magic," said Charlie. "And I believe it. If a magician built this place, why wouldn't he put in all kinds of tricks and illusions, for the fun of the guests? Over all the years, I'm sure many of them were forgotten. But Mr. M. is a magician himself. He'd know what to look for."

Charlie led them back to the intersection of the two corridors. He carefully examined one of the corners. "Look!" he said triumphantly. "This pulls out!"

Ty gripped a small handle hidden in the wooden moulding of the corner's edge. Out came a panel as tall as the wall itself. Smoothly, it glided over to the opposite corner, forming an angle in the corridor. The secret panel was a single, huge mirror.

"Another magic trick," said Ty.

From where the two boys had stood at Miss Drake's apartment, it looked as if they were staring straight down the corridor. But instead, the mirror was reflecting the side corridor, the real one that Mr. Madagascar had run down. He had thrown himself out of the side window and safely landed on the ledge. But the mirror had tricked his small audience into believing he had jumped out of the other window and disappeared.

"It's still a good trick," said Dotty Drake, sadly.

"A magnificent trick!" boomed a voice behind them.

Mr. Madagascar stepped out from Miss Drake's apartment.

11 Misdirection

Mr. Madagascar walked up to Ty and Charlie. "A man jumps out a window and disappears fourteen floors above the ground. Good one, huh?" said the magician.

"Uh, yeah," Charlie said.

"This was supposed to be the beginning of my comeback," Mr. Madagascar said. "I wanted to perform one last show, one astounding trick that would go down in the history books."

"So you planned all of this?" asked Ty.

"Of course I did," said Mr. Madagascar. "I

waited for you to come up to my apartment, and I wanted you to follow me. I had everything all set up. And the lovely Miss Drake here helped by providing some misdirection." He winked at Dotty, who blushed.

Misdirection like Brack performed earlier, thought Charlie. *When he pointed towards the lobby and said, "Now you see him, now you don't." He made us turn around so he could close the two fake mirror walls in the elevator.*

"Your scream was the misdirection," said Ty.

"I always had a good voice for that," Miss Drake said proudly, putting her hand to her throat. "And while I screamed and fainted, the mirror wall slid back into the corner. It's on a timer."

Ty laughed. "So the guy who knocked me down was me!" he said. "My own reflection." He flexed his muscles and added, "I knew he looked tough."

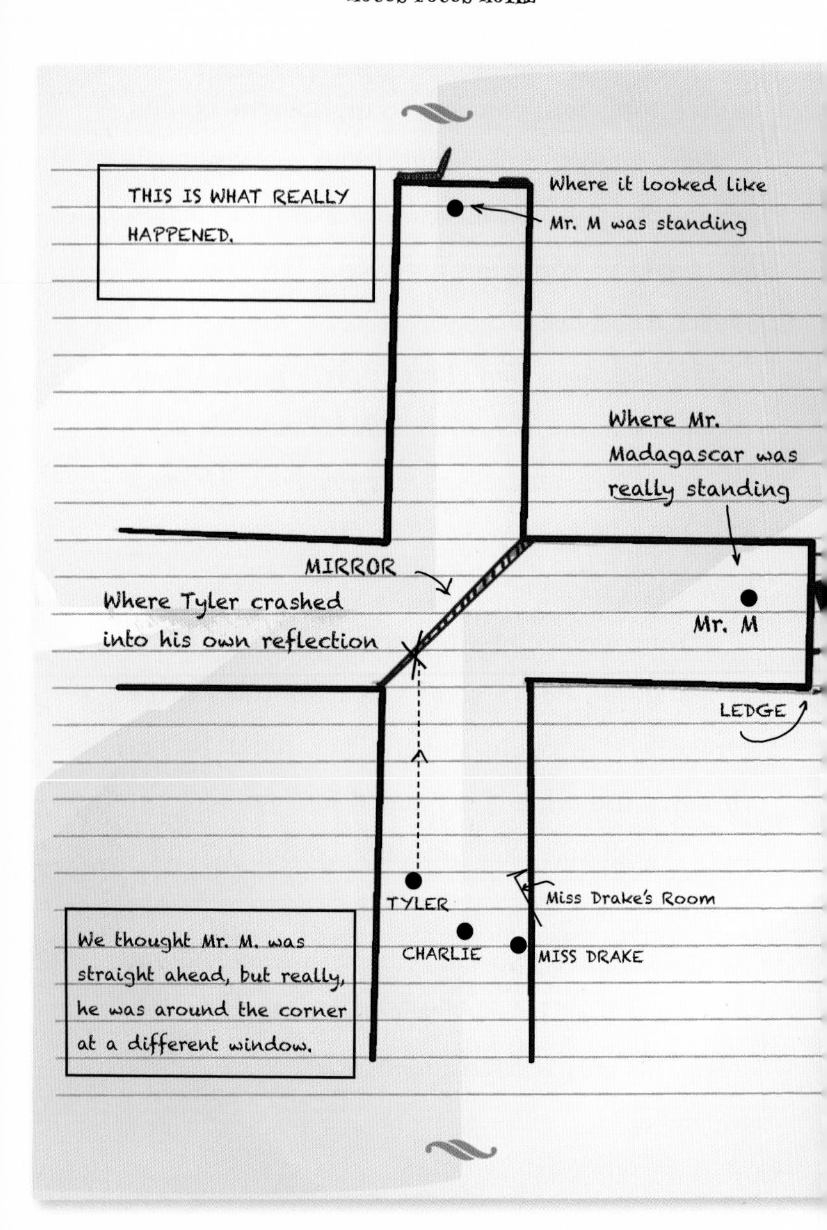
THIS IS WHAT REALLY HAPPENED.
Where it looked like Mr. M was standing
Where Mr. Madagascar was really standing
MIRROR
Where Tyler crashed into his own reflection
Mr. M
LEDGE
TYLER
Miss Drake's Room
CHARLIE
MISS DRAKE
We thought Mr. M. was straight ahead, but really, he was around the corner at a different window.

A low hum rumbled in the hallway. The mirror glided back into the corner and snapped into place. And outside the building, a siren wailed.

"I didn't break any law," said Mr. Madagascar.

"But the police will want to know what—," began Ty.

"Do they have to know tonight?" asked the magician. "Give me twenty-four hours. Give me time to have the headlines proclaim my trick to the world. Then I will reappear, and make a statement to the press."

"And you'll have the best publicity in the world," said Charlie, smiling.

"Exactly," said Mr. Madagascar. "Publicity. And then I can plan my final performance and end with the window trick."

The magician and the former assistant looked at the boys. "My fate – our fate – is in your hands," said Mr. Madagascar.

Ty glanced over at Charlie, and then back at the magician.

"As long as I get this month's rent," Ty said.

"Deal!" exclaimed Mr. Madagascar. "Now come to my room and I will give you your cash."

Ty pumped his fist in the air. "Yeah," he said. "Slamhammer!"

Mr. Madagascar looked confused, but he put his fist in the air too. "Indeed, Slamhammer!" he said.

12 More secrets

The next morning proved Mr. Madagascar and Miss Drake right.

Newspapers, TV stations, and online channels were full of the mysterious disappearance of the magician from the Abracadabra Hotel's fourteenth floor.

Everyone was talking about it, trying to solve the puzzle. There was even a new website – How Did He Do It? – where people posted their own solutions to the mystery.

True to his word, Mr. Madagascar reappeared at the hotel later that day. He gave a press conference that afternoon, and explained that he would soon perform the trick before the eyes of the public, in one last final show of magic.

Of course, everyone at Blackstone Middle School was talking about it. But they were more interested in an even more amazing event.

That morning, when Tyler Yu and Charlie Hitchcock returned to school, it was Tyler who was covered with bruises and cuts. Charlie, on the other hand, seemed perfectly fine.

"Unbelievable," said Charlie's best friend, Andrew, as they sat down to lunch. Everyone in the cafeteria was staring at Charlie. "You are the only person to beat up Tyler Yu!"

Charlie looked up from his lunch. "Who said I beat him up?"

"But just look at him," said Andrew. "You obviously won the fight."

"Don't always trust what you can see," said Charlie.

* * *

That day, two secret notes changed hands.

In the break between English and History, Charlie and Ty each shoved a note in the other's hand.

No one saw.

Ty read his note in his seat at the back of the classroom.

I solved the puzzle of the moving elevator.

Brack's elevator on the 14th floor (#3)

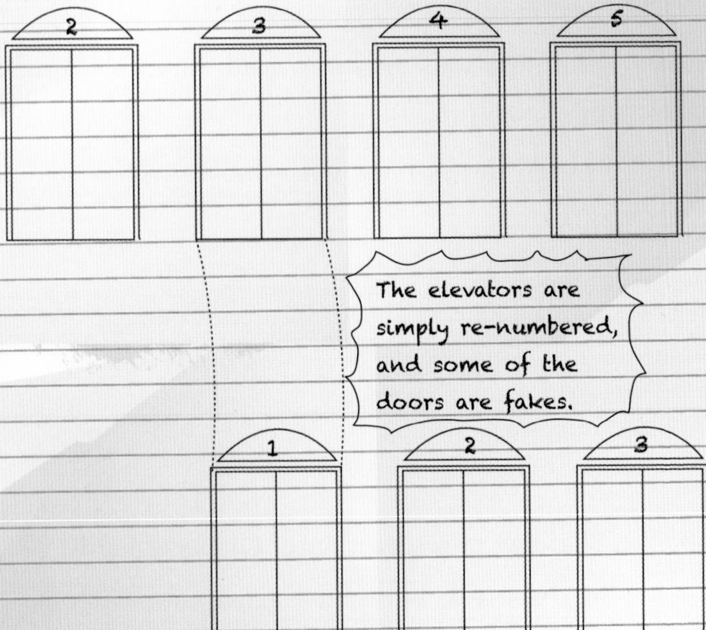

2 3 4 5

The elevators are simply re-numbered, and some of the doors are fakes.

1 2 3

Brack's elevator on the 1st floor lobby (#1)

Just thought you 'd want to know.

HITCH.

At his own desk, Charlie unfolded his note.

DON'T TELL ANYONE ABOUT ME RUNNING INTO THE MIRROR. OR ELSE.

I WONDER IF YOU'RE SMART ENOUGH TO HELP ME WITH ANOTHER SMALL PROBLEM.

I THINK THE HOTEL HAS A GHOST.

13 Zombie eyes

A few days later, Charlie and Ty stood once more in the vast, shadowy lobby of the Abracadabra Hotel.

Outside the building, an October thunder-storm crashed and boomed. Lightning flashed, lighting up the giant painting that hung on the lobby wall. The lightning reflected off Abracadabra's dark shiny eyes.

Zombie eyes, thought Charlie.

Tyler glanced over and asked, "You're not spooked, are you, Hitch?"

Charlie put his hands in his pockets. "Oh, no," he said, rolling his eyes. "I'm standing in an empty lobby in a creepy hotel in the middle of a thunderstorm, and you just told me that there's a ghost floating around here. Why should I be spooked?"

He turned and looked out the hotel's glass doors. Sheets of rain fell on the street and pavement. "I'm going to get soaked when I go home," he said.

"When did you tell your parents you'd be home?" asked Tyler.

"Uh, I didn't say," Charlie said.

"Good," said Tyler. "Then come on. I'll show you the room where the ghost struck first."

"But why do you think it's a ghost?" asked Charlie. "I mean, did someone see a spirit or something?"

"It's because of the voice," said Tyler.

"Voice?" Charlie repeated. Without meaning to, he shivered. He hoped Tyler didn't notice.

"And because of stuff disappearing," said Ty. "And because of what Mr. Thursday said."

Why did I let myself get dragged into another mystery with Ty? wondered Charlie.

Because it was another puzzle?

Because he was afraid Tyler would pound him into the dirt if he didn't help him?

Or some other reason?

"My mum doesn't believe in ghosts," said Ty. "She thinks I'm making up excuses for not wanting to go to the ninth floor. And if I don't find the missing stuff, it comes out of my pay."

Charlie knew what no pay would mean.

If Tyler didn't get paid, he couldn't buy the Tezuki Slamhammer 750, Edition 6, in cherry-pop lightning red.

But making you pay for things that had disappeared, when it wasn't your fault – that didn't seem fair to Charlie.

"What does your dad think about the ghost?" Charlie asked.

"He doesn't go up to the ninth floor either," said Ty. "Especially since he heard the voice."

Thunder crashed, and Charlie jumped. Tyler noticed, but he didn't say anything. He didn't even grin. Instead, he simply said, "Come on, Hitch."

The taller, dark-haired boy led the way across the lobby, past tall marble columns and tall potted palm trees. A row of elevators lined the back wall. Their shiny metal doors shone like gold. Charlie pressed the button to call one.

"Dang!" said Ty. "Wait here. I have to grab the passkey." He spun around and sprinted towards the lobby desk.

"Hey, take my backpack and put it behind the counter," said Charlie.

"I'm not your assistant," said Tyler. As he rushed away, his shoes made wet prints in the thick, blood-red carpet.

"Master Yu is always in a hurry," said Brack, his elevator doors sliding open.

"He knows I can't stay that long," said Charlie.

"Are you helping him solve another mystery?" asked Brack.

Charlie swung his backpack onto one shoulder. "I guess so," he said.

"What draws you to the mysteries here at the Abracadabra?" Brack asked.

Charlie shrugged. "I like puzzles," he said. "Well, actually, I hate puzzles. They bug me until I figure out the answer."

Brack nodded thoughtfully. "Then prepare to be bugged," he said. "Our hotel is full of puzzles. It was designed that way. Riddles and mysteries are built in the walls."

No kidding, Charlie thought.

Just then, Tyler appeared back at the elevator, breathing hard. "Got it," he said, holding up the key. "Ninth floor, Brack."

Thunder shook the building.

"Hey, Mr. Brack," said Charlie. "You don't believe in ghosts, right?"

"Believe in them?" replied Brack. "Of course I do. Why, I've seen them." He pushed a button, the golden doors shut, and the elevator shot upwards.

14 Haunted bathtubs

The boys were stunned. "You saw a ghost?" said Tyler.

Brack nodded. The elevator hummed and shuddered as it rose towards the ninth floor.

"Where did you see it?" asked Charlie.

"In the elevator," answered Brack. He pointed a finger towards the shining gold doors. "I had just dropped off a customer on twelve, and was coming back down to the lobby. And then I saw Abracadabra the magician standing right there, staring at me."

The magician from the painting, thought Charlie.

"Did he say anything?" asked Charlie in whisper.

"Not a syllable," said Brack sadly. "And when I reached the lobby, he disappeared."

"Wow," said Tyler.

"But I've seen him many times since," added Brack.

"On the ninth floor?" asked Ty.

"On many floors," said the elevator operator.

The elevator stopped. Charlie watched his and Ty's reflections, with their mouths hanging open, disappear as the doors slid open. A dark corridor lay beyond.

"You don't have to leave right away, Brack," said Ty. "We won't be long."

"I'll wait as long as I can, Master Yu," said the older man. "But if I hear someone else ring the bell, I'll have to go."

Tyler nodded. He and Charlie started down the corridor, leaving the elevator operator behind. "It's Mr. Thursday's room," said Ty. "Just around the corner, 909."

At the first door around the corner, Tyler shoved the passkey into the lock.

"Don't you knock first?" asked Charlie.

"Relax," said Tyler. "We moved him to a different room after the ghost thing happened. It was easy since he didn't have any luggage. The airline lost it or something."

"Oh," said Charlie.

After stepping inside, Tyler flipped on a light. "The bathroom's over here," he said.

The bathroom was as big as Charlie's bedroom. Marble counters, fancy mirrors, a

shaggy white rug, and a huge bathtub fit inside with plenty of room left over. "Notice anything missing?" asked Tyler, crossing his arms.

"Yes," said Charlie. He stared at the bare curtain rod that hung across the tub. "The shower curtain."

"Score," said Tyler. "The same night Mr. Thursday checked in, he heard a noise in the middle of the night. He said that at first he thought it was a fire. Then as he listened some more, he said it sounded like someone crumpling up paper. And it was coming from the bathroom."

Creepy, thought Charlie.

"Creepy, huh?" said Tyler. "And when he got up to look, he switched on the light, but no one was there. And the shower curtain was gone."

"The room door was locked?" asked Charlie.

Tyler nodded. "From the inside."

"Had he seen the curtain before he went to bed?" asked Charlie.

"Yes," said Ty. "He said he took a shower when he first got in. Then he went and had dinner."

"Ah, and that's when the curtain was stolen!" said Charlie.

"Uh, no," said Tyler. "He said that when he got back to the room, he brushed his teeth before he went to bed. The curtain was still there when he was brushing his teeth."

"Why would someone want a shower curtain?" said Charlie.

"Especially a ghost," added Tyler. "They don't need to take showers."

"He didn't take a shower," said Charlie, "he took a shower curtain. And I still don't see why you think it's a ghost."

"Who else could get into a locked room?" Tyler asked, throwing up his hands. "Who else could remove a solid shower curtain without opening the door?"

"Hmm. Maybe Mr. Thursday did it himself and he's lying," said Charlie.

"I thought of that," said Tyler. "I'm not stupid. I searched the room. It wasn't here."

Maybe he threw it out the window, Charlie thought. *But why would anyone do that?*

"And he couldn't have thrown it out the window, because the room windows don't open," said Tyler.

Charlie stared at him. "How did you know I was thinking about that?" he asked.

"I saw you glance at the window with a funny look on your mug," said Tyler. "And the first time I came in here, that's what I thought too." A smirk spread across his face. "I'm not so dumb after all, am I?"

"I never said you were," said Charlie. In fact, he was really starting to think that Tyler was pretty smart. It was just that Tyler never showed he had brains while he was in school. At school,

Tyler pretty much only showed off his big arms and fists.

Tyler ran a hand through his spiky black hair. "It's crazy," he said. "I just don't get it. Oh, and by the way, this isn't the only room where the shower curtain disappeared."

Tyler led Charlie to five more rooms on the same floor, opening each one with the hotel's passkey. In each room's bathroom, the shower curtain was missing. Only the metal rings that once held the room's curtain in place still dangled on the curtain rod.

"The maids found these," said Tyler. "They always check out the rooms once a week, even if no one has used them. Just to make sure everything is in place."

"So no one is staying here?" Charlie asked.

Ty shook his head. "Nope," he said. "Get this," he added. "None of these rooms has had a guest for over a week. They've been empty. And the cleaning people all swore the shower curtains were still there when they cleaned them."

"They couldn't have made a mistake?" asked Charlie.

"No way," said Tyler. "The cleaning crew has a checklist for each room. If anything is missing, they have to report it. My mum's a real stickler for being organized and clean."

"Six rooms without shower curtains," said Charlie.

"There's other stuff missing, too," said Tyler. "Now we need to go downstairs."

"There could be more than one ghost," said Charlie.

Suddenly, they both froze. A moan echoed through the dim corridor.

"There it is!" whispered Tyler. "The voice."

Mr. Ken

A name was being called out over and over. "Mister Ken . . . Mister Ken . . ."

The voice was soft, but clear. "See what I mean?" said Tyler quietly. He motioned for Charlie to walk down the corridor with him.

Even as they tiptoed past door after door, the voice seemed to follow them.

Charlie tapped Ty's back and whispered, "Where's it coming from?"

Tyler shook his head. "I can't tell. I've put my ears to the doors on this floor, but it isn't coming from inside anywhere. It's out here, in the hall."

"Mister Ken . . . Mister Ken . . ."

The voice sounded angry. When it wasn't speaking the man's name, it was merely moaning.

"You go down that corridor," said Tyler, pointing. "I'll go down this way."

Charlie nodded and headed down the corridor. He wished he had a torch in his backpack. Even with a flash of lightning through the hall windows now and then, it was not easy to see his way down the corridor.

The ancient wallpaper was decorated with big black flowers.

Lilies? wondered Charlie.

The carpet was a deep green. The hall lamps

were small and old-fashioned, covered with dim red shades.

It reminded Charlie of walking through a funhouse. Or a creepy hotel in a scary movie. He half expected to see ghostly kids each time he turned a corner. But, except for Tyler, he was the only other person walking the corridors.

Neither of them saw a ghost or a moving shadow or a floating orb of light. They made a circuit of all the corridors on the ninth floor. They passed the row of elevators twice (Mr. Brack was gone by then). And though the voice was equally clear throughout the corridors, they still couldn't tell where it was coming from.

For a while, Charlie thought that Ty was playing a trick on him. Firstly, Charlie didn't believe in ghosts, so he had a hard time believing that the biggest bully in school did. Secondly, he could easily imagine Tyler telling his bully buddies how he had pranked Charlie and freaked him out.

But after several minutes of prowling corridors, Charlie could tell that Ty was nervous too.

Every time they passed each other, Tyler would ask, "Anything?"

Charlie would shake his head and say, "You?"

Tyler would shake his head. And the two would keep walking.

Charlie did notice that the voice seemed to change volume as he walked. It would grow softer and then louder as he walked down a hall. If he retraced his steps to where the sound had been soft, it grew softer once more.

Weird, thought Charlie.

Charlie noticed something else. A second sound. It was softer than the mysterious voice, but always there in the background. A tinkling sound, like a tiny silver bell.

Suddenly, the voice grew rougher, heavier. There was a loud bang.

The voice cried out one more time, and then – silence.

"Wow," said Tyler, walking up to Charlie.

"So, who's this Mister Ken guy?" asked Charlie.

"Beats me," said Ty. "He could be a magician, maybe? They always call themselves Mister this or Mister that. I wonder if he used to live here a long time ago and maybe died in the hotel."

"Or maybe it's the ghost of Abracadabra," added Charlie.

"Let's ask Brack, when his elevator gets here," said Tyler. "He knows everything about this place."

"Maybe there's a record of accidents that happened here," said Charlie. "We could Google it, I bet."

He pushed the button for an elevator, but when the next one came, it was not Brack's.

"No problem," said Tyler. "We need to go back downstairs anyway."

As they stepped inside the elevator, Charlie

thought about the ghost that had shown itself to the elderly operator. Something about Brack's story didn't sound right.

16
The missing

When they reached the first-floor lobby, Tyler led Charlie past the front desk and down a broad flight of steps. At the bottom, they walked through several more corridors and finally came to a huge room with a shiny wooden floor.

"You have a bowling alley down here?" exclaimed Charlie. His voice echoed in the large, empty space.

"Yup," said Tyler. "With nine lanes. But it's closed now because of the ghost."

"Don't tell me he stole the bowling balls," said Charlie.

"No, the pins," Tyler said. "Not all of them. Just nine. One from each alley."

"This is getting weirder by the minute," said Charlie.

"And it's not over," said Ty.

As he led Charlie back towards the marble steps, they passed another door. Actually, it was a set of double doors. Charlie noticed that the carved wooden doors were each decorated with a face. One face was smiling, and one was frowning.

"What's that?" Charlie asked.

"Oh, that's the old theatre," said Tyler, sounding bored.

Charlie darted over and peered inside the doors. It was another huge room, bigger than the bowling alley. Rows and rows of red velvet seats faced a large stage. The stage curtains looked about a mile high. They were pulled to the sides, so that the shiny wooden floor of the stage could be clearly seen. It was one of the most amazing rooms Charlie had ever seen.

Charlie rubbed his hand along the back of one of the theatre chairs. "Cool," he whispered.

"No one's used this place for years," said Tyler. "This is where they used to have the old magic shows. Come on, let's go."

He led Charlie back up the stairs and into the hotel's main floor restaurant, the Top Hat.

Several of the tables and booths were already filled with hungry guests. At the back of the dining area was the kitchen. Warm air and chattering voices greeted the boys as they passed through the kitchen's swinging doors.

"Hey, Dad!" yelled Ty.

A tall man wearing a tall white chef's hat hurried over to meet him.

"Tyler, you shouldn't be back here," said Mr. Yu. "Only cooks and waiters."

"I know, I know," said Tyler.

"Who's this?" asked his father, gesturing towards Charlie. "Your friend from school?"

"Yeah, this is Hitch," said Ty. "He's here because he's interested in the ghost."

"Ah," said his father, nodding his head. "Our phantom friend."

Charlie noticed that the older Yu had the same eyes as his son. But his face was much friendlier. *Tyler must get his scowl from his mum,* thought Charlie.

"Tell him what the ghost took from your kitchen, Dad," said Tyler.

"I don't know if it was a ghost," said Mr. Yu, smiling. "But someone took half a dozen of my best serving spoons."

"The big kind," added Tyler. "You know, for scooping out stuff."

"We run a tight ship here at the Top Hat," said Mr. Yu. "Every pot, pan, plate, and utensil is accounted for. I can't understand why anyone would want serving spoons."

"Are they valuable?" asked Charlie.

"Well, they are old," admitted Mr. Yu. "And I'm sure they're genuine silver. They came with the original silverware from the hotel's first restaurant."

"Think they're worth a hundred bucks, Dad?" asked Tyler.

"Probably more," said Mr. Yu. "Now, I need to get back to my customers. We're serving one of my specialities tonight, Flambeau de Chesterton. I have to make sure I don't set off the fire alarm like I did last time. You boys have fun."

"See you later," Tyler said.

"Nice to meet you," Charlie said.

Mr. Yu smiled at him. Then the boys left.

As they returned to the lobby, Charlie stopped and asked, "Why do you think a ghost stole the spoons?"

"Not so loud," whispered Tyler. "I don't want the guests to hear. It's bad for business."

He grabbed Charlie by the collar and pulled him into a shadowy corner, where they were surrounded by potted palms and giant ceramic vases.

"There's no one around," said Charlie, readjusting his collar.

"Yeah, but that lobby echoes," said Tyler. He shrugged. "My family has a reputation to uphold here."

"So tell me why you think—" Charlie began.

"Yeah, yeah, the ghost," said Tyler. "Definitely took the spoons. And I think so because it all happened the same night. After Mr. Thursday called us upstairs about the shower curtain, that same night, my dad noticed his spoons were gone. And later, my mum got complaints from some of the guests that the bowling pins were missing downstairs."

"That is weird," said Charlie.

"No kidding," said Tyler. "This is why you need to solve the mystery. And it'd better be quick, before something else disappears."

Just then, a hand reached out from behind one of the giant vases.

17
Finding the key

Tyler jumped as the hand grabbed at him.

"Where's my key?" came a voice.

As the mysterious hand moved closer to Tyler, Charlie saw that it was attached to an arm, then a shoulder, then an entire body of a teenage

boy with long blond hair. He was wearing a dark maroon suit and a gold name badge.

"Don't do that!" said Tyler.

"Sorry, man," said the teenager. "I need my passkey back." He turned and looked at Charlie. "Who are you?"

Charlie began, "I'm —"

"He's Hitch," said Tyler. "And here's your stupid passkey." He handed it to the blond guy, who shoved it in his pocket.

"Your mum was looking for it," said the blond guy. "And I don't want to lose it like last time."

"You lost it?" Charlie asked.

The blond guy turned to Tyler. "Who is this kid?" he asked. "And why does he care about my stupid passkey?"

"I'm, uh, writing a report on the hotel for school," said Charlie. "Who are you?"

"Rocky," said the guy. "I work the front desk."

"He and Annie switch off," explained Tyler.

"When did you lose the key?" Charlie asked.

"I didn't really lose it," said Rocky. "I just misplaced it. I was checking people in and I had a lot on my mind. I couldn't find the key, but when I looked again a little later, there it was on the floor. Must have dropped it. Anyway, why do you care when I lost it?"

"Don't you have work to do?" asked Tyler.

"Nice talking to you too, Ty," said Rocky. He pushed his long hair behind his ears and walked back towards the desk.

"Well, that could explain our ghost," said Charlie.

"What could? Rocky?" asked Tyler.

"No, the passkey," said Charlie. "Rocky said he was missing it for a little while, right? So while it was gone, someone could have used it to get into the rooms on the ninth floor and steal the shower curtains."

"You're right," said Tyler.

"And does the passkey let you into the bowling alley and the kitchen?" asked Charlie.

"Yeah. It unlocks every door in the hotel," said Tyler.

"So that's how the thief did it," said Charlie. "Stole the spoons and shower curtains and everything."

"But how could you steal a key right in front of someone?" asked Tyler. "Rocky's not that smart, but he does notice things. He knew you and I were over here behind these plants and vases."

"Right," Charlie said. "That's why I think it had to be a magician."

"Why?" Tyler asked.

"Magicians use the trick I'm thinking of all the time," said Charlie. "It's called palming. It's how they can hide an object in their hands, right under your nose. Or they distract you, make you look at something else, while they put the object in their pocket."

"Hmm," said Tyler. He strode across the lobby and stopped at the front desk. Rocky was busy working at a computer.

"Hey, Rock," said Tyler. "The day you couldn't find that key, were there lots of people checking in?"

"I'm busy here, Ty," said Rocky.

"Just tell me what you dropped on the floor that day," said Tyler.

"Just someone's credit card and . . . hey, how did you know I dropped something?" Rocky asked, turning from the computer.

"Elementary," said Tyler, with a smirk. "Whose card was it?'

"And when did all this happen?" added Charlie.

Rocky thought for a moment. He brushed the hair out of his eyes and said, "It was Thursday."

"PALMING"

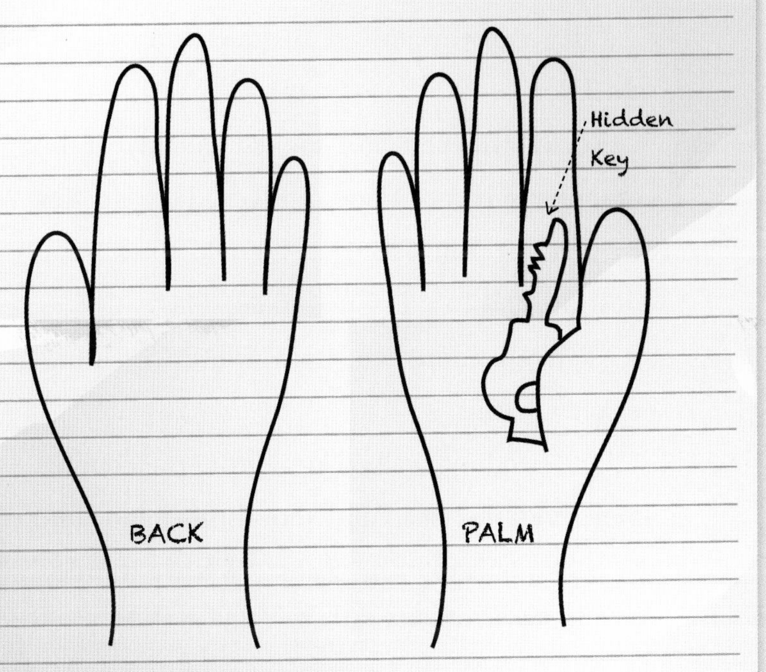

A magician palms, or hides an object in the palm of his hand, by grabbing onto it with the fatty part of his thumb.

"Thanks, Rock," said Tyler.

Then Charlie asked, "And were any of those people you checked in named Ken?"

"You're starting to bug me, kid," said Rocky.

"Hey, can you answer his question or not?" said Tyler.

Rocky frowned and looked quickly at his computer screen. "Nope, no Ken. Hey, no Ken do. Get it? You asked if I could answer his question, and I said, 'No Ken do.' Ha."

"You're a comedian," said Tyler. "Come on," he told Charlie.

The two boys walked away from the counter. Tyler shook his head and shoved his hands into the back pockets of his jeans. "What a weirdo," he mumbled. "Well, now what do we do?"

This puzzle was more bizarre than the Mr. Madagascar one.

This was more than just a magician trying out a fancy trick. This mystery had a ghost, a wavering voice, missing bowling pins, spoons, and shower curtains. What did bowling pins have to do with ghosts? What did silver spoons have to do with shower curtains?

Or maybe not exactly shower curtains, Charlie thought. There was something he had seen in Mr. Thursday's bathroom that he hadn't seen in the others Tyler had shown him.

The other thing, the weirdest thing, was that Charlie was sure there was a phantom cleaner in the hotel. Things were being cleaned without anyone else realizing it.

Suddenly, grunts echoed through the lobby. Charlie turned and saw a couple of men walk towards the counter where Rocky was working. Rain dripped from their clothes and their shoes.

The men had thick necks and broad shoulders, but they were struggling with two huge suitcases. They set them down by Rocky, then took out handkerchiefs and wiped their foreheads.

"Thanks," Rocky said.

"We got one more," said one of the men. He jerked his thumb over his shoulder towards the front door. An empty taxi was sitting by the kerb.

Charlie looked at the suitcases again. Things were starting to make sense to him.

"I think we need to go back up to the ninth floor," said Charlie. "There's something else missing from the bathroom in Room 909."

18
The echo

"I don't hear the voice," said Tyler.

"Me either," Charlie said. "Just wait."

They were walking through the corridors again on the ninth floor. When they reached Room 909, Tyler unlocked the door with the passkey. He'd grabbed it while Rocky was busy with the heavy suitcases that had just arrived.

"Okay, Hitch," said Tyler. "What's the deal with Mr. Thursday's bathroom?"

"Look at the curtain rod," said Charlie. "See anything?"

"Uh, no," replied Tyler. "I already told you that the ghost, or whatever it was, stole the shower curtains."

"Right," said Charlie. "But I remember something from the other bathrooms. Since I have acute visual memory, I remember . . ."

"Yeah, yeah, I know," said Tyler, with a frown. "You remember everything you see."

"And the other rooms don't match this room," Charlie said.

Tyler frowned, but he took off and ran to one of the other hotel rooms.

Charlie followed as Tyler rushed inside the other room and disappeared into the bathroom.

"Wow!" came his voice.

"See it?" asked Charlie.

Tyler walked slowly out of the second bathroom and stared at Charlie. "You did it again, Hitch," he said. "This bathroom has the curtain rings still attached."

"They all do," said Charlie. "Except for the curtain rod in Mr. Thursday's bathroom. The shower curtains and the rings are missing."

"But why?" asked Tyler. "What's the difference?"

"Let's see, there are about twelve or so rings on each rod," Charlie said thoughtfully. "Someone wanted those rings."

"They're not valuable," said Tyler. "Just made out of metal."

Ooooooh-oooooooohhhhhh!

The boys stared at each other. The voice had returned.

"This guy is starting to tick me off," growled Tyler. He rushed out of the room and strode down the corridor.

"Where are you?" he called out. "What's your problem?!"

Charlie followed him, listening closely to the phantom sound.

"Mister Ken . . . ahhhh . . . uhhh . . . Mister Ken . . ."

The moan echoed through the corridor.

"Wait here," said Charlie.

He rushed back to the corridor where he had earlier noticed the ghost's voice growing softer. Yes, it was still soft in that area.

Charlie walked down the hallway until the voice seemed louder again.

There has to be a logical explanation, he thought.

He dropped his backpack onto the carpet and knelt down. He fished through one of the pockets to find his notebook and a pen. He wanted to write down all the clues they had discovered so far.

Then he noticed something. When he was kneeling down on the floor, the sound was louder.

What is going on? he thought.

Staying on his knees, he crawled to one side of the hall. No, the sound was normal. Then he crawled to the other side. The voice was louder.

Charlie stared at the dark wall. The wallpaper design of big black flowers stretched all the way to the floor. But in the dim light, Charlie could see that there was a small vent disguised in the black petals. He pressed an ear to the vent and heard the ghostly voice loud and clear.

He sat up and called out, "Hey, Tyler! Come here!"

Tyler rushed into the corridor. "You saw it?" he asked.

Charlie shook his head. "No," he said, "but I heard it." He pointed at the vent. Tyler bent down and listened closely. They both heard Mister Ken's name cried out again.

"I know where it's coming from," Tyler said suddenly.

"Where?" Charlie asked.

Tyler shuddered and said, "The basement!"

Behind the boilers

On the way downstairs in the elevator – this time, it was Brack's – Charlie made a quick list on his notepad of the clues and questions they had.

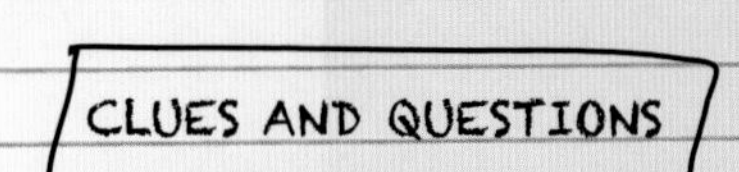

1. Missing spoons, curtain rings, bowling pins → (why would one person want all three of these objects?)

2. Other shower curtains missing on Floor 9 → EXTREMELY WEIRD

3. A ghostly voice in the vent

4. Who (or what) is Mister Ken?

5. The lost passkey ??

6. Heavy luggage turning up at the counter

"You have the hunter's gleam in your eye, Master Hitchcock," said Brack. "Do I detect that you have solved the puzzle?"

"He better have solved it," muttered Tyler.

Charlie grinned and told Brack, "Well, I've solved at least part of it."

Leaning in to look at Charlie's list, the operator raised an eyebrow. "So you have juggled all your clues and evidence together," he said, "and that's why you are travelling to the basement?"

"We always end up in the basement," said Tyler.

"But the mystery was solved upstairs on the ninth floor," said Charlie. "Down here we'll find out who's behind the mystery."

The elevator stopped and the doors slid open. "Good luck," said Brack. "I hope your solution turns tragedy into comedy."

As the elevator doors closed behind them, Tyler looked down at Charlie and said, "That guy is always saying weird stuff."

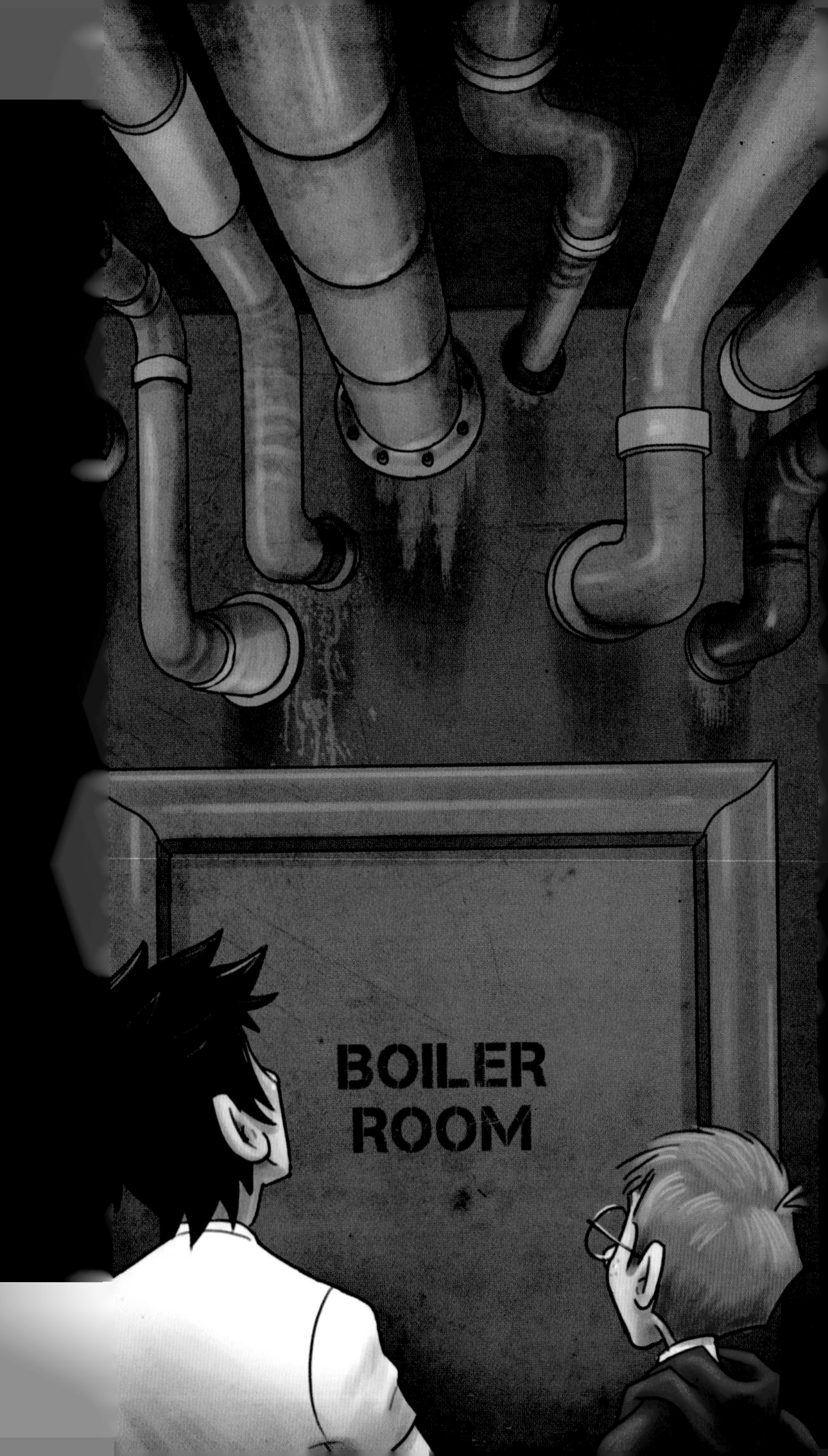
BOILER
ROOM

Weird, but full of clues, thought Charlie. *Tragedy and comedy?*

"I think he's pretty smart," Charlie said. "Anyway, where should we go?"

Tyler shrugged and pointed. "This way," he said. "Follow the pipes."

Long metal ducts snaked across the ceilings. As they walked deeper into the basement, more and more of the ducts appeared from different directions. They connected and joined together, forming even bigger pipes, and all running in the same direction.

They all passed through a wall near an orange door labelled BOILER ROOM.

When they opened the heavy orange metal door, Tyler and Charlie were met by a blast of thick, warm air. All the ducts entered this room. Half of them flowed into the dozen metal boilers. The boilers heated air. Then the air was carried by the other ducts to the vents on all the hotel's floors.

"If someone could be heard through that vent," whispered Tyler, "then they must be somewhere in this room."

Charlie grabbed Tyler's T-shirt. "Look! Over there!" he said.

A man's shadow covered one of the room's cement walls. His hands fluttered up and down in a strange way, as if he were brushing aside spider webs. Or as if he were a magician casting a spell.

His hands stopped. "Mister Ken," they heard him say. Then the man's shadow disappeared.

20
Mr. Thursday

"Hurry!" said Tyler. "Before he disappears!"

The boys dashed around the row of boilers. A young man turned abruptly, a surprised look on his face. He was surrounded by nine bowling pins. A heap of metal spoons and rings was lying at his feet. Behind him lay a neatly folded shower curtain.

"You're the ghost!" accused Tyler angrily.

"Ghost?" repeated the man. "What are you talking about?"

"He's not a ghost," said Charlie. "He's a juggler."

"Juggler?" repeated Tyler.

"Mr. Thursday, right?" asked Charlie.

The man bowed towards them. "Thursday the Master Thrower," said the juggler. "And I'm sorry about taking these things. But I had to practise."

"And your luggage was lost by the airlines," said Charlie. "Along with your usual props, like bowling pins, juggling rings, and metal rods."

"Exactly," said Thursday. "I just borrowed these items to use until mine turn up. I always planned to return them. I even folded the shower curtain!"

"Your luggage just got here," said Charlie. "We saw it up in the lobby."

"Slow down," Tyler said. "What's going on?"

"He's another performer," explained Charlie. "Like the magicians who live here. And just like any performer, he has to practise every single day."

"But why do you practise down here?" asked Tyler.

"Because the ceiling's high enough," said Mr. Thursday.

"So we were hearing you practise through the vents," said Tyler. "The vents next to this wall must go right up to the ninth floor. So, who is this Mister Ken guy?"

"Mister Ken?" Mr. Thursday said. "Who's that?"

Charlie smiled. "He wasn't saying Mister Ken," he said. "We just thought he was. I finally figured it out when I realized what all three objects had in common."

"What do you mean?" Tyler asked.

Charlie explained, "I was thinking, 'What would someone use rings, spoons, and bowling pins for?' Then I thought, 'Of course! Juggling!' Then I realized that what we were hearing was Mr. Thursday rehearsing his act."

"What does that have to do with Mister Ken?" Tyler asked.

Charlie smiled again. "There is no Mister Ken," he said.

"Okay, I really don't get it," Tyler said.

Charlie said, "Whenever he dropped a spoon or ring or pin, he would say to himself, 'Missed again, missed again.' That's what we were hearing. We just thought he was saying Mister Ken, but he was giving himself a hard time for screwing up while practising."

Thursday blushed above his beard. "It's a bad habit of mine," he said.

"It just sounded like 'Mister Ken,'" said Charlie.

"I have to practise every day, otherwise I get rusty," said Thursday. "I would have asked to use these things, but it was supposed to be a surprise."

"A surprise for what?" asked Tyler.

"For the magic show," said Mr. Thursday. "Of course."

21 The final mysteries

"Wait a second," Tyler said. "What magic show? I haven't heard about any magic show."

"A magic show like the ones the Abracadabra had in the old days," said Thursday. His voice was full of excitement. "And you haven't heard about it because it's a surprise," he added. "The magicians here are all organizing it."

"Wow!" said Tyler. "Mum will be so excited about all this. She'll love it!"

"Do me a favour," Thursday said. "Keep it a surprise, for now. There are going to be a few shows coming up. The big one will take us a while to prepare."

"Got it," Tyler said. Charlie nodded.

Thursday rubbed at his beard. "Uh, you don't mind if I keep practising, then, do you?" he asked.

"What? Oh, no, knock yourself out," said Tyler. "But it would be better if you used your own stuff, since it's here. Can you help me take these bowling pins back upstairs?"

"No problem," said Thursday.

* * *

Later, after Charlie, Tyler, and Mr. Thursday had returned the missing objects to their rightful places, Charlie stood in the lobby next to the front doors. It was still raining outside.

He stared at the tall painting of the former Abracadabra, the hotel's founder. He was studying the magician's eyes.

Tyler walked up to him. "Hey, you might want this," he said. He handed Charlie an umbrella. "People always forget theirs when they leave the hotel, so we have lots of extra ones lying around."

"Thanks," said Charlie.

"No problem," said Tyler. "Well, so it wasn't a ghost after all. And Mum won't deduct my money now to pay for the missing stuff."

"Great," said Charlie.

"Well, see you at school," said Tyler. He started to walk away. But then he stopped, turned, and added, "But remember, don't talk to me in the halls."

Charlie nodded and smiled. At school, he was the brain. Tyler was the bully. Everyone had their separate place at school. No one would ever suspect them of working together. But in the magicians' hotel, it was as if they became new people.

When Tyler had disappeared into his family's living quarters, Charlie hurried over to the row of elevators. He pushed the button.

Just as he had hoped, the elevator on the far left opened.

"Going up, Master Hitchcock?" asked Brack.

22 The penthouse

Charlie stepped briskly into the elevator. He watched his reflection in the shiny golden doors as they slid closed.

"This is where you saw the phantom of old Abracadabra, right?" asked Charlie.

"What's on your mind, young man?" asked the operator. The elevator began to rise.

"Puzzles," said Charlie.

"More puzzles?" asked Brack.

Charlie nodded. "Someone stole the shower curtains from the other rooms on the ninth floor," he said.

"So I hear," said Brack.

"But it wasn't Mr. Thursday," Charlie said. "Why would he? He only needed a dozen metal rings for practice. Besides, how would he get inside those rooms?"

"I'm not sure," Brack said.

"Someone who knew how to get the passkey could do it," Charlie said. "Someone who knew how to palm things. Someone who could hang around the front desk and not be suspected. Like an old and trusted employee, maybe?"

"Maybe," said Brack.

"And why would those other shower curtains be taken?" asked Charlie.

"Hmm," said Brack.

"Maybe to throw off suspicion from Mr. Thursday," Charlie said. "Because if his shower curtain was the only one that disappeared, people might investigate him. They might find him in the basement, practising. And that would spoil the surprise of the show."

"Perhaps," said Brack.

"Also, how would Thursday know where to practise his juggling?" Charlie went on. "This was his first time in the hotel. Only someone who knew the hotel like the back of his hand could tell him where to find a great rehearsal space."

"Could be," said Brack.

"And finally," said Charlie. "Who's the mysterious cleaner?"

"What do you mean?" asked Brack.

"The old theatre," Charlie said. "The floor of the stage has been recently swept. Maybe mopped. It was shiny. That doesn't make any sense at all! It should have been dull and covered with dust."

"Why do you think that?" asked Brack.

Charlie shrugged. "Tyler said no one had been in the theatre for years," he said. "So it shouldn't have been clean. If anyone had been in there, he certainly would have heard about it. Since he hears about everything. I even rubbed my hand along the back of one of the seats. It was clean too. Someone was getting the theatre ready for a show."

"Incredible," said Brack.

"And of course, I remembered certain things you said to me when Ty and I got off the elevator," said Charlie. "You said I had juggled the clues together. Mr. Thursday turned out to be a juggler."

"Isn't that interesting," said Brack.

Charlie nodded. "Then you said you hoped my solution to the ghost mystery would turn tragedy into comedy," he went on. "The faces carved into the doors of the theatre are the famous faces of Tragedy and Comedy. I've seen them before. You can find them in lots of theatres. They're an old tradition."

"You know a lot of things, Master Hitchcock," said Brack.

"I read a lot," said Charlie. "And I have—"

"An acute visual memory," finished Brack. "I know."

"You know a lot, too, Mr. Brack," said Charlie. "Your words to me in the elevator proved it. You knew what was going on all the time."

"I keep my ears and eyes open," said Brack.

"Someone is putting on a show," said Charlie. "Like the shows in the olden days."

"Is that so?" Brack said, a twinkle in his eye.

"Yes," Charlie said. "You know all about it. Thursday was invited to be part of it. Mr. Madagascar, up on the thirteenth floor, is planning on his comeback."

"So I've heard," Brack said.

"I'm guessing Mr. Madagascar is probably going to be in the magic show too," Charlie said.

"Perhaps he is," Brack said.

"And who better to plan a magic show like the old days than a magician from the old days? And who better from the old days than the greatest magician of them all?"

"Who indeed," Brack said.

"Abracadabra," Charlie said.

Brack smiled. "You would make a good magician yourself, Master Hitchcock," he said. "How did you solve this mystery?"

"Lots of little things," said Charlie. "But I really started thinking about it when you told us you saw the ghost here in your elevator. You pointed, and I looked at where you pointed, at the shiny doors."

"Aha," said Brack. He smiled.

"I saw my reflection in the doors," Charlie explained, "and that's when I started to put the pieces together."

"Of course," said Brack. "I am impressed, Master Hitchcock."

"When you look at your reflection, you see a ghost from the past," Charlie said gently. "You see Abracadabra."

"Yes, yes," said Brack. "It's the eyes. Hair turns grey and falls out, ears grow bigger, wrinkles attack your skin. But a person's eyes stay the same."

"Just like the painting in the lobby," said Charlie. "That was my final clue."

"I could never leave the hotel," said Brack. "It's my home. And I feel protective of the other magicians here. We don't have many places left, magicians. Not the ones from the old days, anyway. So I decided on this new disguise, this new identity."

"And a new name," Charlie said.

Brack smiled. "Yes," he said. "And a new name."

"Brack is short for Abracadabra," said Charlie. "I guessed that, too."

"You guessed very well," said the magician. "And you seemed to have solved all the puzzles. Well done. So I guess this is for you."

Brack pulled a gold card from his uniform pocket and handed it to Charlie. Charlie looked down at it.

"Thank you, Mr. Abracadabra," said Charlie, holding the golden ticket.

"My pleasure, Master Hitchcock," said Brack.

The elevator stopped.

The doors slid open.

Beyond, Charlie saw the roof of the hotel. Trees bloomed in concrete planters. Flowers were planted in careful paths. There was a stone walkway that led to a stone house, with small, warm windows and odd-shaped towers.

Charlie knew without being told that it was Brack's house.

"Would you care for a cup of hot cocoa?" asked the magician.

"But who'll operate the elevators?" asked Charlie.

"It's all automatic," said Brack, smiling. "I don't think anyone will mind if the hotel's two puzzle masters take a short break."

Charlie opened his umbrella, and the magician and the boy walked towards the house.

ABOUT THE AUTHOR

MICHAEL DAHL grew up reading everything he could find about his hero Harry Houdini, and worked as a magician's assistant when he was a teenager. Even though he cannot disappear, he is very good at escaping things. Dahl has written the popular Library of Doom series, the Dragonblood books, and the Finnegan Zwake series. He currently lives in the Midwest of the United States, in a haunted house.

ABOUT THE ILLUSTRATOR

LISA K. WEBER is an illustrator currently living in California in the United States. She graduated from Parsons School of Design in 2000 and then began freelancing. Since then, she has completed many print, animation, and design projects, including graphic novelizations of classic literature, character and background designs for children's cartoons, and textiles for dogs' clothing.

The premiere

On Friday at three o'clock, Tyler Yu and Charlie Hitchcock stood together just inside the back doors of Blackstone Middle School.

Each of them clutched a packet of paper. All around them, other students took books from their lockers, packed their bags, and made plans for the weekend.

It was an ordinary Friday afternoon. There was nothing at all unusual about the scene.

Except that Ty was the biggest bully in school, and Charlie was best known for his photographic memory, and they weren't supposed to be friends.

"Okay," Ty said. "This is where we split up."

Charlie nodded.

"I'll hand out flyers to the eighth-graders," Ty went on. "I'll also hand out flyers to the jocks, the cool kids, the cheerleaders, and the crew in detention."

"Who does that leave for me?" Charlie asked, looking up at Ty.

"The dorks," Ty said. He shrugged. "And the nerds."

Charlie rolled his eyes. "Don't forget the geeks."

"Them too," Ty agreed. He pointed towards the science wing. "You go that way."

"Obviously," Charlie said. He walked off into the crowd.

"And remember – you don't know me," Ty called after him.

Charlie reached the first corner and stopped. Then he turned and saw Ty, across the main corridor, handing some sheets of paper to two eighth-grade girls.

"I think they'll figure out that we know each other," Charlie hollered, "when they realize we're handing out the same flyers!"

Smiling, he headed down the science corridor. He would never have tried something like that a few weeks ago, but ever since Charlie helped Ty solve two magic mysteries at the Abracadabra Hotel, the two boys had become something like friends.

Ty would probably deny that.

Actually, Charlie was sure Ty would deny that.

But he knew it was true.

Thirty minutes later, the boys met up at the front of the school. All the flyers were handed out, except one, which Charlie still held in both hands.

"Why did you save that one?" Ty said. "Did you give one to every kid?"

Charlie nodded.

"Chess club?" Ty asked.

"Yup," said Charlie.

"Computer club?" Ty asked.

"Of course," said Charlie.

"What about the chemistry club?" Ty suggested.

"Got 'em," Charlie said. "I promise. I got everyone. This one is to hang up."

Charlie led the way to the office bulletin board. He handed the flyer to Ty. "Hold this," he said. Then Charlie pulled two tacks from his pocket, took the flyer back from Ty, and tacked it into place on the bulletin board.

"There," Charlie said. The boys stood back and looked at the flyer.

is proud to present

ITS FIRST MAGIC SHOW
IN FIFTY YEARS

TWO SHOWS THIS SATURDAY
12 NOON AND 7 P.M.

FEATURING

MADAME KRZYSCKY, THE FIRE-EATER
MIND-READING HYPNOTISM BY
THE GREAT PROFESSOR PONTIFICATE
THE AMAZING MR. THURSDAY, JUGGLER
AND ALL THE WAY FROM THE LOST KINGDOM OF GILJARRI . . .
EXPLORER OF MAGICAL REALMS . . . MASTER OF DIMENSIONAL POWERS
BEYOND YOUR WILDEST IMAGININGS . . .
THE GREATEST PERFORMER OF OUR AGE OR ANY AGE . . . .

THE GREAT AND POWERFUL
THEOPOLIS!